Written by Jane Clarke
Illustrated by Sarah McConnell

Collins

All Hughie does is chew, chew, chew.
Whatever are we going to do?

He chews up toys, he chews up bones.

He chews up shoes and mobile phones.

He chews his bed, he chews his bowls.

He chews up all our toilet rolls.

He chews our dirty underwear.
Chewy Hughie doesn't care.

He chews the paper and the mail.

When Mum says “NO!”, he wags his tail.

He chews the chairs and both settees.
He chews our books and DVDs.
He chews the carpets and the doors.
Nothing's safe from Hughie's jaws.

Whatever are we going to do?
All Hughie does is chew, chew, **chew**.

Outside, he chews up grass and trees,
flowers, flies and bumblebees.

He chews up Grandad's stick and hat ...

... he tries to chew up Granny's cat.

Mum says, “Keep an eye on Hughie!”

He’s in my room, but he’s still chewy.

He's found a pack of bubble gum.

Hughie's chewing it for fun.

All Hughie does is chew, chew, chew ...

... now his jaws are stuck like glue.

Chewy Hughie's in big trouble.
He's inside a huge, pink bubble.

Hughie, you have got to stop.

Don't chew, Hughie, you'll go ...

POP!

Now Hughie doesn't chew, chew, chew.

Whatever is he going to do?

A story map

Ideas for guided reading

Learning objectives: use a variety of cues to predict and check the meanings of unfamiliar words and to make sense of what they read; identify and describe characters, expressing own views and using words and phrases from the text; identify and discuss patterns of rhythm, rhyme and other patterns of sound; speak with clarity and use intonation when reading and reciting texts; blend to read words containing a large range of vowel digraphs and trigraphs

Curriculum links: Citizenship – Animals and us

Interest words: chewy, whatever, mobile phones, underwear, settees, bumblebees, bubble gum

Word count: 206

Getting started

This book may be read over two sessions.

- Referring to the title, ask the children to predict what the problem might be in this story. Discuss the rhyme in the title and find another rhyming word in the blurb. Ask them to predict the 'something special' that Hughie will find.
- Skimming quickly through pp2-13, ask the children to discuss with a partner the kinds of things Hughie likes to chew. They could take turns to name things they see in the artwork or text.
- Return to pp2-5 and show how to read pp2-5 using rhythm. Allow each child to practise this. Praise clarity and expression.

Reading and responding

- As the children read aloud individually, listen in and praise use of a range of strategies to problem-solve.
- After a few pages, pause to discuss Hughie. *What kind of character is he? How would you describe him? Disobedient, naughty, energetic?*